WELCOME TO

RAVENS PASS

WITCH MAYOR

by Steve Brezenoff
illustrated by Tom Percival

Ravens Pass is published by Stone Arch Books
a Capstone imprint
1710 Roe Crest Drive
North Mankato, Minnesota 56003
www.capstonepub.com

Library of Congress Cataloging-in-Publication Data
Brezenoff, Steven.

Witch mayor / written by Steve Brezenoff ; illustrated by Tom Percival.

p. cm. -- (Ravens Pass)

Summary: Hank and Gus want to investigate the legend that the Ravens Pass city hall was built over a cellar with a witch sealed inside it, and a school field trip seems like the perfect opportunity--but the witch may be waiting for them.

ISBN 978-1-4342-3791-0 (library binding) -- ISBN 978-1-4342-4212-9 (pbk.) -- ISBN 978-1-4342-4655-4 (ebook)

1. Witches--Juvenile fiction. 2. Women mayors--Juvenile fiction. 3. Women teachers--Juvenile fiction. 4. School field trips--Juvenile fiction. 5. Horror tales. [1. Witches--Fiction. 2. Mayors--Fiction. 3. School field trips--Fiction. 4. Horror stories.] I. Percival, Tom, 1977- ill. II. Title.

PZ7.B7576Wi 2012

813.6--dc23

2012003962

Graphic Designer: Hilary Wacholz
Art Director: Kay Fraser

Photo credits:
iStockphoto: chromatika (sign, backcover); spxChrome (torn paper, pp. 7, 15, 23, 29, 37, 43, 49, 55, 63, 73, 79, 83) Shutterstock: Milos Luzanin (newspaper, pp. 92, 93, 94, 95, 96); Robyn Mackenzie (torn ad, pp. 1, 2, 96); Tischenko Irina (sign, pp. 1, 2); Photographic textures and elements from cgtextures, composited by Tom Percival: (front cover and pp. 11, 18, 25, 34, 39, 45, 52, 60, 69, 75, 81, 89, 93)

Printed in the United States of America
in Stevens Point, Wisconsin.
042012   006678WZF12

Between where you live and where you've been, there is a town. It lies along the highway, and off the beaten path. It's in the middle of a forest, and in the middle of a desert. It's on the shore of a lake, and along a raging river. It's surrounded by mountains, and on the edge of a deadly cliff. If you're looking for it, you'll never find it, but if you're lost, it'll appear on your path.

The town is **RAVENS PASS**, and you might never leave.

TABLE OF CONTENTS

Chapter 1

THE VILLAGERS

Though it was early afternoon, the sky was as dark as midnight and full of thick, low gray clouds. The rain fell across the village's main street. It was hardly a street at all, really, mostly dirt and gravel and far too much mud.

The villagers stomped through the mud. They carried whatever weapons they could find: pitchforks, garden hoes, ropes, and chains. Several people carried torches, but in the gusting wind and violent rain, the flames didn't stay lit.

The crowd marched to the new City Hall. The building wasn't even finished yet. Ravens Pass had only been founded a few days before.

And already, it was in grave danger.

They reached the new stone foundation. The cellar had been dug. It had been lined with great rocks from the riverbed at the edge of the new town.

The middle of the cellar was still uncovered by the main floor. Really, it was little more than a great big hole in the ground. And inside it stood a woman. She watched the crowd approach.

They'd come for her, she knew, but she was not afraid. In her hands she held a glowing ball. No one remembered what it was made of—glass or stone or something else entirely.

But it didn't matter, that no one remembered. Because really, the ball was made of raw, dark power.

The woman held the sphere up over her head as the villagers approached. Then she spoke a dark, deep incantation.

The villagers heard her, even over the crashing thunder and gusting winds. They stopped to watch. Their lanterns flickered and went out. The few torches that had survived this long fizzled and smoked.

The skies opened with a great thunderous boom. Lightning burst across the sky, and rain fell in sheets.

The witch, with the glowing orb still in her palms, rose from the sunken earth and floated slowly toward the crowd.

They screamed. They ran in every direction. Most didn't make it far.

They tripped. They slid in the muddy street. They dodged falling trees in the storm and strikes of lightning. One woman still stood, and she faced the witch. Her pitchfork had broken, and she held the long handle in front of her.

"How dare you?!" the witch exclaimed. She landed before the woman standing alone.

"You cannot begin to understand my power," the witch said. She lifted the orb, and it glowed even brighter. The witch began to chant again, but as she opened her mouth, a bolt of lightning slammed down from the heavens.

It connected with the orb, knocking the witch back—back into the cellar, into the gathered mud and water from the storm.

She sank quickly.

The clouds parted. The storm stopped. The villagers who could still stand ran to the edge of the cellar and looked in.

"We must work quickly," said the woman who had faced the witch. "We must finish the building now, on top of the witch, before she wakes."

And so they did. The villagers worked all night, and through the next day, and the next, until Ravens Pass City Hall was finished. They all vowed never to let another soul enter that basement.

No one thought Ravens Pass would be founded through such tragedy. But the surviving villagers, though they were tired, cheered for the woman who had stood up to that witch.

And that day, they honored her.

They gave her a job that would let her watch over the children of Ravens Pass.

Chapter 2

CITY HALL

Aug. 3

"That's the most ridiculous story I've ever heard," said Gus Jerome. He sat on the top rung of the monkey bars in Ravens Pass's only playground. Since the playground sat right on the edge of the cemetery, most kids didn't go near it.

Gus had listened carefully to his friend Hank's story about the witch, trapped for centuries in the basement of Ravens Pass's City Hall. It was no coincidence, of course, that the next day, Gus and Hank's sixth-grade class would be going on a field trip to City Hall themselves.

For years, City Hall hadn't been open to the public. But the city had recently decided to start inviting school field trips. Hank and Gus's class would be the first group of people allowed into the building in hundreds of years.

"You don't have to believe me," Hank said. He swung lazily between two bars under Gus, his feet dragging in the pebbly sand. "But tomorrow, I plan to go down to the cellar to find her."

Gus laughed. "First of all, you're crazy," he said. "For one thing, even if the story were true, that witch would be dead by now."

Hank shook his head. "Witches don't die," he said. "Unless you light them on fire, or pour water over them, or something like that. So that witch is definitely still alive, and she's definitely still in City Hall."

Gus rolled his eyes, but he laughed. "Second of all," he said, "Ms. Freckle is going to be watching you like a hawk. Remember the trouble you caused on the trip to the ketchup factory?"

"That wasn't my fault!" Hank protested, stomping his feet in the sand. "How was I supposed to know Brittany Wilder was standing under the ketchup chute?"

"Tell it to Ms. Freckle," Gus said. "Either way, she won't let you out of her sight at City Hall tomorrow. You won't make it near the cellar door."

"That's why you have to help me," Hank said. "If you cause a distraction—"

Gus shook his head and waved his hand. "No," he said firmly. "No way. I am not helping you with this. It's stupid."

"Come on," Hank said. "I'll tell you what. I'll give you . . ."

Gus looked down at his friend, who was sneering up at him. He obviously had a good offer planned. Gus swung down and dropped to the sand. He stood in front of Hank in the middle of the monkey bars.

"Okay, what?" Gus said.

"The Sword of Kal'hya," Hank said. "It's yours. If you help me tomorrow."

"Um, Hank?" Gus said, turning around and ducking out of the monkey bars. "The Sword of Kal'hya isn't real. It's a weapon from a video game." Specifically, it was one of the best swords from Battle Knights, an online game the boys played all the time.

"Yup," Hank said, "and I found it while I was playing last night."

"What?" Gus said. "Why didn't you tell me?"

"I just did," Hank said. "But if you want it, I will give it to you for free."

"Seriously?" Gus said. "That sword is worth, like, two thousand gold, probably."

"That's right," Hank said. "That should show you how serious I am about getting into that cellar tomorrow."

Gus couldn't say no. He tried for a minute. He knew how much trouble he could get into. These schemes of Hank's never ended well. The last time he helped Hank with one of his plans, they both ended up in detention, stapling four thousand handouts for a third-grade class. It took two weeks of staying after school.

But he wanted the Sword of Kal'hya. With that sword, he could defeat every other player in the game, and every monster in every dungeon. How could he say no?

Gus put out his hand. "Deal," he said, and he and Hank shook on it. Gus began to regret it right away.

Chapter 3

FORMING A PLAN

The mayor's assistant, Hubert Pommel, greeted the class at City Hall the next day. "If you children will follow me," he said, after pointing out the exits and restrooms, "we will begin our tour in the meeting hall."

Ms. Freckle clapped her hands twice, very quickly. The sharp sound echoed through City Hall's marble entryway. "Chop chop!" she said. "Follow Mr. Pommel, children."

The class fell into two single file lines, marching side by side behind Mr. Pommel. Ms. Freckle walked behind them.

Ms. Freckle was a strict lady. She was one of the strictest teachers in school. Gus knew she was just watching out for them, and that she wanted the best for them. But sometimes it got pretty annoying to have to follow her directions all the time and act like you were in the army or something.

Gus and Hank made sure to get in different lines, toward the middle, so they could talk without Ms. Freckle or Mr. Pommel overhearing.

"Have you decided how to distract Ms. Freckle yet?" Hank whispered.

Gus nodded once.

"More importantly," Gus said, "have you transferred that sword to my character yet?"

"Heck no," Hank said, a little too loudly. "Not yet."

From the back of the line, Ms. Freckle hissed through her teeth. "Not a peep, class!" she snapped. "You must listen to me—you all know it's my job to protect you."

Gus rolled his eyes. Ms. Freckle was always saying that. Like her students really needed protecting.

Hank continued in his quietest whisper. "I'll transfer the sword after you've fulfilled your part of the bargain," he said.

"No way," Gus said. "Transfer it first. In fact, do it right now."

"Don't you trust me?" Hank said.

"Not at all," Gus said. He smiled.

Chapter 4

THE WRONG KEY

"Fine," Hank said. He glanced over his shoulder at Ms. Freckle, and then looked at Mr. Pommel at the front of the line.

The group was still moving down a long windowless hallway, toward the back of the building.

Hank pulled his phone from his pocket. He tapped the screen a couple of times as Gus looked over his shoulder.

Gus really wanted a phone like that, but his parents wouldn't let him get anything fancy. His phone was just so they could find him, and he could find them, in an emergency. No games. No videos. And definitely no apps to connect with Battle Knights.

Gus watched Hank's finger slide across the screen. It pulled the sword—a shimmering blue blade that sparkled under a gold and silver halo—from Hank's account to Gus's. "There," Hank said. "Happy?"

Gus smirked. "I'll be happy when you hit save," he said.

"Oh yeah," Hank said. His face went red. "I forgot."

He tapped the little save button, and then slipped his phone back into his pocket.

At the same instant, Mr. Pommel stopped. Then the class stopped behind him.

Mr. Pommel cleared his throat. "This," he said in a loud and important voice, "is the meeting hall. It is empty now, which is why we can go in."

He turned around and put his hand on the knob. He wiggled the knob. It didn't turn. The door was locked.

Mr. Pommel smiled. "Um," he said, stammering a bit. "Let's see. . . ."

He dug in his pocket. Finally, with some jangling and jiggling, he pulled out his key ring, full of keys.

"I'll just unlock this door now," Mr. Pommel said, fumbling with the keys. He tried one in the lock, but it didn't work. "Whoops, wrong key," he said. "I thought it was a silver one. Hmm. . . ."

Gus stood on his toes for a better look. Mr. Pommel's key ring must have had a hundred keys on it. This could take all day.

He put up his hand. "Yes, Gus?" Ms. Freckle said.

Gus turned around to face her. "May I use the restroom, ma'am?" he said.

The teacher smiled. Gus knew Ms. Freckle absolutely loved it when her students called her ma'am, and used "may" instead of "can."

"Of course," Ms. Freckle said with a big smile. "Do you know where it is?"

"Yes, ma'am," Gus said. "Mr. Pommel was kind enough to point it out when we arrived."

Ms. Freckle looked for a moment like she might pass out with joy.

While she was still smiling and beaming all over the place, Gus winked at Hank. Then he stepped away from the line and walked back down the long hallway.

The bathroom was on the other side of the front lobby. Gus's sneakers squeaked and chirped as he crossed the marble tiled floor.

On the way, he stopped to look at the bronze statue standing in the middle of the lobby. The statue was of a very tall and very serious-looking woman.

Her strong jaw and wide mouth made her seem powerful, like nothing could stop her.

"There are hard times ahead," her stance seemed to say, "but I will lead the people of Ravens Pass safely through them, to a golden age!"

In one hand, she held a cane—more like a staff, really. A pair of spectacles dangled from the fingers of her other hand.

A velvet rope stopped him from getting too close, but he could read the plaque. It read, "Ravens Pass's first mayor, Kathrin Verteidiger."

Gus got a last look at the statue's face. Then he turned and headed for the bathrooms. Between the men's room and women's room was an unmarked door.

Maybe that's the cellar door, Gus thought. He tried the handle. It was locked.

"Can I help you?" a voice said.

Gus spun. A woman stood there. She wore glasses and held a long cane in one hand, and she looked identical to the statue.

Chapter 5

MEETING THE MAYOR

Gus stared at the woman. "I—I—" he stuttered. "You—you're—"

The woman smiled and pulled off her glasses. She slipped them into the chest pocket of her blazer. With her glasses off, she looked even more like the statue.

"I am Mayor Kate Verttiger," she said. Then she tapped the tip of her cane on the marble floor, very lightly.

Gus couldn't help staring at the cane. Its tip and top were shiny silver, and its wood looked old. Ancient, even—old enough to have been around at the time Ravens Pass was founded.

"And who are you?" the mayor asked.

"I'm with a field trip," Gus said. "I was heading to the bathroom."

The mayor stood and faced the statue. "And you stopped to admire this statue," she said. "I don't blame you. She was a very interesting woman."

"Was?" Gus said. "She's not you? I mean, you're not she? I mean—"

The mayor laughed. "Of course not!" she said. "This is my great-great-great-grandmother. She founded this town two hundred years ago." The mayor leaned over and looked into Gus's eyes. "Do I look as old as that?" she said, grinning.

"No," Gus said. "Of course not. Ma'am." He turned away.

Her stare made him feel cold. A chill ran up his spine and his shoulders shook. "Excuse me," he said. "I better get going. My teacher will be annoyed that I've been gone so long."

He started back toward the long hallway where his class was. But Mayor Vertigger called after him, "Didn't you have to use the restroom?"

"Oh yeah," Gus said, feeling silly. He hurried through the lobby, jogging past the mayor. He kept his eyes on the floor the whole time.

As Gus passed her, the mayor smiled. "One more thing," she said in her icy voice.

Gus cleared his throat. "Yes?" he said, still not looking at her. He kept his eyes on her feet instead.

"Stay away from the cellar," the mayor hissed.

"Yes, ma'am," Gus said.

"And make sure your friends stay away, too," she added.

Gus nodded. Then he hurried from the lobby and into the restroom.

"See you later!" called the mayor. Her voice was like ice in Gus's blood.

Chapter 6

9.66
31.96 0.02 ь.4 14.2 |

THE WITCH?

TTLE
·5

"Finally," Hank said when Gus joined the class again. Mr. Pommel had finally gotten the meeting hall door open, and the class was shuffling into the room.

"Yeah," Gus said. "Took a while."

"Did you set something up?" Hank asked.

Gus shook his head. His face was still wet because he'd splashed it with water in the bathroom. It was the only way he could calm down. "No," he said. "I didn't."

Hank frowned. "What have you been doing, then?" he asked.

"I can't help you," Gus replied. "You can have the dumb sword back. It's not worth it."

"What do you mean?" Hank asked. The two boys stayed in the back of the hall, since Ms. Freckle went up to the front with Mr. Pommel.

"I mean I don't want any part of your investigation," Gus said. He watched as Hank pulled out his phone and opened the Battle Knights app again.

He poked at the screen a few times. "You have to sign in," Hank said.

"Fine," Gus said. He took the phone and started to sign in. Suddenly, though, a bony old hand snatched the phone away.

"Aha!" Ms. Freckle said. She held the phone behind her back.

Hank's face fell. "Oh, no," he muttered.

"I expect this sort of thing from Hank," Ms. Freckle said. "But I'm disappointed in you, Gus. Such a polite young man." She shook her head and clucked her tongue. Then she went back to the front of the hall to stand with Mr. Pommel again. Mr. Pommel was rambling on about the town's history.

"Well," Hanks said quietly, "I guess we're both in trouble now."

Gus nodded. "Might as well investigate, then," Hank went on.

Gus glared at him. "It's not Ms. Freckle I'm worried about," he said. "It's the mayor."

"The mayor?" Hank repeated. "Did you see her?"

"Yeah. In the lobby," Gus said. "I think maybe she's the witch."

He hadn't even realized it till he said it out loud, but it made sense. That was why the mayor had freaked him out so much.

She wasn't just the first mayor's descendant. She was the first mayor.

She was the witch.

Chapter 7

BROKEN OUT

Gus explained his theory to Hank. The mayor looked exactly like the woman in the statue, and that was because she WAS the woman in the statue.

She hadn't aged a day since she got trapped in the mud and flood in the cellar. And the chill she sent up his spine—she must be a witch.

She'd broken out of the cellar.

Hank listened closely. He nodded slowly, like it made sense.

"Of course," he said when Gus was done. "I can't believe I didn't think of it before. No old cellar door is going to trap a powerful witch for long. But I bet she hasn't even left City Hall."

"What about that other woman?" Gus said. "Why isn't she here to protect us?"

Hank shook his head. "Don't you get it?" he asked. "She wasn't a witch. She would have died like a hundred and fifty years ago." He laughed. "She'd be as old as Ms. Freckle if she were still alive."

They glanced at their teacher. She was standing near Mr. Pommel at the front of the room. He was finishing his speech about early government in Ravens Pass.

Even Ms. Freckle looked bored, standing there. She checked her watch.

"Now," Mr. Pommel said, "if you'll all follow me, we'll take a look at the records room. I'm sure you'll find it quite fascinating."

Hank put up his hand, and Mr. Pommel pointed at him. "Yes?" Mr. Pommel said.

"Will we get to meet the mayor herself?" Hank asked.

Gus rolled his eyes and elbowed his friend. "What are you doing?" Gus snapped.

"Shh," Hank whispered. "I'm just asking, sheesh."

"The mayor's office is on the tour today, yes," Mr. Pommel said. "Mayor Vertigger is looking forward to meeting all of you children today. She's thrilled that we've opened City Hall to the public. Her office will be your . . . very last stop."

As he said the words "your last stop," Mr. Pommel smiled. His toothy grin—it looked too big for his face—gave Gus another shiver.

"Mr. Pommel must work for her," Hank whispered. "And not just as a mayor's assistant, either."

"What do you mean?" Gus said, but he had a hunch he already knew.

"He knows," Hank said. "He knows she's a witch."

Gus swallowed. "And our class," he said, "is about to be her first victims in two hundred years."

Chapter 8

NEW PLAN

Aug. 3

"We have to get out of here," Gus told Hank.
His voice shook.

They were in the records room, and Mr.
Pommel had finished his records-room speech. It
was mostly about the first citizens of Ravens Pass,
and how they all died of some horrible disease, and
how those who hadn't died had fled.

The way Mr. Pommel told the story, the mayor
had been basically all by herself in Ravens Pass, and
due to her hard work, the town survived.

Some parts of the story reminded Gus of Hank's creepy tale about Ravens Pass's founding. But Mr. Pommel left out anything about a witch.

"So where did the rest of us come from?" Hank asked. "If the witch was the only person here, I mean."

"Who cares?" Gus said, gritting his teeth. "If we stay on this tour, we're doomed."

Hank's face got serious. "What should we do?" he finally asked.

Gus looked around.

The other students all stared at Mr. Pommel as he rambled on. Their mouths hung open. Gus thought a few of them might be sleeping with their eyes open. He didn't blame them. He'd be bored too, if it weren't for the witch mayor.

He had to figure out what to do. He knew adults were supposed to be the ones you went to in emergencies, but Ms. Freckle would be no help. She was looking down her nose and over her glasses at the class, just waiting for someone to breathe wrong or cough, so she could give them detention.

Gus and Hank would have to save the day.

"We have to stop this tour," Gus said. "It's not enough for us to escape. If we stop the tour, we'll save the whole class."

"Okay," Hank said, keeping an eye on Ms. Freckle. "How do we do that?"

Gus looked around the big records room. It was mostly full of tall, wooden file cabinets that looked like they'd been built before the Civil War.

Then he spotted something that was obviously much newer: a red switch on the wall near the door.

The fire alarm.

He grinned.

Hank followed Gus's gaze with his own. "Got it," Hank said. "I'll make sure no one notices. You go hit the alarm."

Hank didn't wait for Gus to reply. He just reached into his pocket and pulled something out. Then he raised his closed fist and heaved the thing, whatever it was, toward the corner of the room.

There was a loud pop. Mr. Pommel stopped his speech. The whole class turned to look where the thing had popped.

"Go," Hank hissed.

Gus didn't wait around any longer. He hurried to the door and grabbed the red switch. But as he did, the little stinkbomb Hank had thrown began to erupt in green and gray smoke. The room filled with a terrible stink.

Gus pulled the handle. The fire alarm blared.

Students shrieked. Gus watched Ms. Freckle and Mr. Pommel at the front of the room. His teacher put up her hands and tried to calm the class.

Mr. Pommel looked mad. Then he started to look worried.

"Everyone, please move toward the exit," Ms. Freckle said. Gus was kind of impressed with how calm the teacher was.

The students were all panicking.

Even Mr. Pommel seemed to panic. Gus watched him from the door as he waited for the rest of the class and Ms. Freckle to leave. Hank stood on the other side of the door, and together they encouraged the rest of the class to stay calm.

But Gus also watched Mr. Pommel. He stayed at the back of the records room. Then, when the mayor's assistant thought no one was paying attention, he reached behind one of those old file cabinets and flicked an invisible switch.

A short door, hidden in the corner, swung open. Mr. Pommel ducked inside. The door swung shut, totally silent.

Chapter 9

ESCAPE

"Did you see that?" Gus whispered. "Pommel just snuck out through that little door!"

Hank nodded. "He must be going to warn the mayor," he said. "Her victims are escaping. She won't like that."

Everyone was leaving the records room. Most of the other students were already out.

Ms. Freckle, Hank, and Gus left the records room behind the rest of the class.

"I can't imagine what happened to Mr. Pommel," she said as they hurried toward the front exit. "He should be helping us get out of here."

"I don't think he wants us to escape, Ms. Freckle," Hank said.

"What do you mean?" she asked. "Why wouldn't he want us to get out?"

Gus and Hank exchanged a glance. "Should we tell her?" Hank said.

Gus thought about it. Everyone knew the story of the witch who tried to destroy Ravens Pass before it could even be founded.

Maybe Ms. Freckle would understand—maybe she'd even be able to help them. It definitely couldn't hurt to have a grown-up on their side.

"I think it's okay," Gus said. "Tell her."

"You tell her," Hank said. "You'll explain it better."

"We think Mayor Vertigger is the witch," Gus said in a quick burst. "The witch who tried to destroy Ravens Pass two hundred years ago. You know, from the old story."

They'd reached the front door of City Hall. The class was already streaming onto the sidewalk.

Ms. Freckle stopped and faced the boys. She seemed to be thinking very hard. "I didn't know the children of Ravens Pass still talked about that witch," she said. She seemed pleased.

Then she nodded once, firmly. "It makes sense," she said. "And I suppose Pommel is her assistant." She looked at the statue—the one of the founding mayor, the woman who looked exactly like the current mayor.

Anger flashed across her face.

"And I figure," Gus went on, "the reason no one's been allowed in City Hall for so long is that she was afraid someone would figure out her secret. That's why they just started opening it to the public."

Hank scratched his chin. "I just can't figure out why she let us in," he said.

Ms. Freckle smiled. "Don't you see?" she said. "It's been two hundred years. She needs new sacrifices."

Hank's face went white. Gus felt his stomach churn with fear.

The last student in their class had made it out of the building. Only Gus, Hank, and Ms. Freckle were still inside.

"Let's get out of here," Gus said, "before we become sacrifices."

The three of them turned for the door, but as they did, it slammed closed.

Hank grabbed the handle and tugged and pushed and kicked. "Help! It won't budge!" he cried.

Suddenly a voice came over the public address system. "You will not escape," the voice said. It was Mr. Pommel. "Mayor Vertigger has plans for you," he went on. "She will be arriving at the statue to collect you shortly."

"We have to get out of here," Gus said.

"I couldn't agree more," Ms. Freckle said. Her face went fierce and she clamped a hand on each of the boys' shoulders.

"We have to stick together," she said. "You'll need to listen to me and do as I say. Remember, I'm here to protect you."

The boys nodded. They didn't love the idea of being alone in City Hall with that crazy witch and her assistant anyway.

The sound of the mayor's high-heel boots echoed through the marble halls. "She's coming," Gus said.

Ms. Freckle looked around desperately. She seemed to focus on a plain-looking metal door, near the bathrooms.

"The cellar," she said. It was almost a whisper. Her voice sounded different—tougher, darker. "Come on." She walked quickly toward the plain door. Gus and Hank hurried to keep up.

"I think we're going to be okay," Gus said quietly. "I think Ms. Freckle can protect us."

Hank nodded. "I know," he said. "I feel like that too. Weird, huh?"

At the metal cellar door, Ms. Freckle reached for the handle. "Follow me," she told the boys. "Stay close."

"It's locked," Gus said. "I tried it before."

But it wasn't locked anymore.

The door swung open, and Ms. Freckle motioned the boys inside.

Chapter 10

IN THE CELLAR

It was dark once Ms. Freckle closed the cellar door behind them. A long set of steps led down into the cool and even darker basement. The floor was stone. The walls were stone and damp. It smelled old and musty. The only light came from the very middle of the large empty room.

There, on a stone post, was a single glowing sphere.

"What is it?" Hank whispered.

Gus shook his head. He stayed way back, too.

For some reason, he didn't think it was a good idea to get too near that thing.

From above them, at the top of the steps, there came a click.

"She locked us in!" Hank said. He ran for the steps.

A moment later, Gus could hear Hank struggling with the door handle and banging on the door. He pounded on the wood, but no one opened the door.

"Let us out!" Hank shouted. "Come on! Help! We're locked in here!"

Still, no one came.

Gus watched Ms. Freckle. She was staring at the red light shining from the orb in the middle of the room.

"Maybe we shouldn't have gone into the cellar," Gus said. "Maybe we should have tried to find an open window or something."

But Ms. Freckle didn't seem to hear him. "This is the power," she said.

Her smile grew. Her eyebrows arched. The light from the sphere made her face bright and pink. The light shined off her thick glasses.

Gus gulped. Ms. Freckle was starting to make him nervous, and that sphere seemed pretty dangerous.

Hank kept banging at the door. "Let us out!" he called.

"Ms. Freckle?" Gus said. "I don't think you should get too close to that thing. It—uh, it doesn't seem safe at all."

She ignored him and stepped closer, her hands wide and out in front of her, like she could absorb its light into her skin. "After so long, you will be mine again," she said.

Chapter 11

DANGEROUS

Gus took a step back and stumbled on the bottom step. He could still hear Hank at the top, banging on the door.

"Please," Gus said, standing up. "I think that's hers. It's probably dangerous."

"Of course it's dangerous," Ms. Freckle said. Then she cackled. "But it's not hers. It's not the mayor's."

She laughed again.

Gus grabbed the banister and got to his feet. "Whose . . ." he began, his voice cracking. "Whose is it?"

Ms. Freckle leapt at the sphere and clamped her hands on it. The air crackled with energy and the red and pink glow filled the cellar.

"What's going on down there?" Hank shouted. Gus couldn't even answer. He could only watch.

Ms. Freckle glowed. She seemed to grow taller, and light shined from every pore of her body. Her eyes flashed and flared beams of red light. Every hair on her head was like a cable, waving and flashing, filling the cellar with blinding light.

Chapter 12

SACRIFICES

Aug. 3

Gus scrambled up the steps on all fours as Hank came running down.

"Turn around!" Gus shouted over the explosion of energy from behind him.

"What's going on?" Hank shouted back.

"The witch," Gus said. "It's not the mayor!"

They ran to the top. Together, they pounded on the door.

"But it has to be her," Hank said. "Who else could she be?"

"She's the real mayor," Gus shouted. "Her ancestor was the mayor too—the one who saved the town from the witch. Remember the story?"

Hank stared at him.

"And now Mayor Vertigger is doing the same thing," Gus said. "She's trying to save the town from the witch."

Hank looked over his shoulder, down the steps, into the bright red light of the cellar. The light was brighter now, like it was moving toward them.

"She's coming," he said.

Gus pounded harder on the door. "Let us out!" he cried. "Please, let us out! We're not your enemies!"

The high-heeled boots clipped and clopped just outside the door and stopped.

"We can hear you out there," Gus said. He pressed his face against the cold metal door. "Please, open the door. She's almost here. We can't escape."

"I'm sorry," the mayor said through the door. Gus thought she did sound sorry. "I didn't mean to catch you two boys as well," the mayor said. "But I can't risk opening the door now, not now that the witch is reunited with her power sphere."

"But why?" Hank shouted. "Why did you let her get the sphere?"

"I knew she would come for it," the mayor said. "And now she is trapped in the cellar, where she can do no more harm."

Hank turned his back on the door. "She's coming," he said. He tugged on Gus's arm.

But Gus kept his ear pressed against the door. "Please!" he shouted.

"I'm sorry," the mayor replied. "If it makes you feel any better, you two will be the witch's last victims. You're doing a great service for Ravens Pass."

They heard the clip clop of her high-heeled boots as she walked away from the door.

ABOUT THE AUTHOR

STEVE BREZENOFF is the author of dozens of chapter books for young readers and two novels for young adults. Some of his creepiest ideas show up in dreams, so most of the Ravens Pass stories were written in his pajamas. He lives in St. Paul, Minnesota, with his wife, their son, and their hopelessly neurotic dog.

ABOUT THE ILLUSTRATOR

TOM PERCIVAL was born and raised in the wilds of Shropshire, England, a place of such remarkable natural beauty that Tom decided to sit in his room every day, drawing pictures and writing stories. But that was all a long time ago, and much has changed since then. Now, Tom lives in Bristol, England, where he sits in his room all day, drawing pictures and writing stories while his patient girlfriend, Liz, and their son, Ethan, keep him company.

GLOSSARY

CELLAR (SEL-ur)—a room below ground level

COINCIDENCE (koh-IN-si-duhnss)—a chance happening

DESCENDANTS (di-SEND-uhnts)—someone's children, their children's children, and so on into the future

INVESTIGATION (in-vess-tuh-GAY-shun)—a search to find out as much as possible about something

ORB (ORB)—a solid, round shape

PLAQUE (PLAK)—a plate with words on it, usually placed on a wall in a public place

SOURCE (SORSS)—the place where something begins

SPHERE (SFEER)—a solid, round shape

THEORY (THIHR-ee)—an idea of how something happened

TRANSFERRED (TRANS-furd)—moved from one place to another

VICTIM (VIK-tuhm)—a person who is hurt by someone

DISCUSSION QUESTIONS

1. Explain who each person is in this book.

2. In this series, Ravens Pass is a town where crazy things happen. Has anything spooky or creepy ever happened in your town? Talk about stories you know.

3. Can you think of any other explanations for the creepy things that happen in this book? Discuss your ideas.

WRITING PROMPTS

1. What happens next? Write a short story that extends this book.

2. Imagine that you lived in Ravens Pass when it was founded. What was the town like?

3. Write a newspaper article describing the events in this book.

THE CROW'S

FIELD TRIP GOES WRONG

You may have heard that the City Hall building suddenly stopped hosting field trips last week, right after the big deal the Mayor's office made about letting the public into the building again.

The new official statement from Mayor Vertigger said they changed their minds because of some top-secret government information.

But a mole in the public schools tells me that's not exactly true. Turns out a class went on a field trip to the office after all.

The school is officially denying that, but I've heard rumors around town that a field trip did in fact take place.

And it happened the same day those two boys went missing.

AND BELIEVE US, THERE'S A LOT OF IT!

EYE

Now, we all know the stories about Ravens Pass's beginnings as a town.

There's something very fishy about this.

The Mayor's office was reached for comment, but they said they have nothing more to say on the matter.

I'm keeping my eyes open.

Mayor Vertigger, the day of her official statement.

MORE
DARK TALES

WITCH MAYOR

There's a story going around that the mayor of Ravens Pass is a witch. Could it be true?

CURSES FOR SALE

Weird things happen after Jace buys an old toy car at a garage sale. Is the toy cursed?

THE SLEEPER

The old orphanage on the outskirts of Ravens Pass? It's full of aliens ready to take over the planet.

NEW IN TOWN

When Andy is threatened, a new kid protects him. But there's something very strange about the new kid in town . . .